Tink's Great Idea

~❖ Book Ten ❖~

DISNEP PRESS
New York

Illustrated by the Disney Storybook Artists
Designed by Deborah Boone

Printed in China

First Edition
1 3 5 7 9 10 8 6 4 2

Library of Congress Catalog Card Number on file.

ISBN 978-1-4231-3054-3
F904-9088-1-10144

For more Disney Press fun,
visit www.disneybooks.com

"It's working!" Tink cried. The tinker fairy had rounded up several Sprinting Thistles, Pixie Hollow's wildest weeds. Then Tinker Bell went in search of more. Maybe if she captured them all, Tink thought, she could become a garden fairy and help bring spring to the mainland. Tinker Bell wanted to go to the mainland more than anything! But only nature talents were permitted to make the trip.

Unfortunately, Tink didn't realize that fast-flying Vidia had tricked her. She had given Tink the idea to capture the thistles to prove that she wasn't just a pots-and-pans fairy. But as soon as Tink had gone to find more, mean-spirited Vidia opened the gate and let the thistles out!

As they sprinted away, the escaped thistles were joined by other thistles. More and more appeared until they formed a sprinting-thistle stampede! Tinker Bell couldn't believe her eyes. She knew the weeds spelled trouble for Pixie Hollow!

The thistles trampled everything in their path—from Sunflower Meadow to Flutterby Forest. Then, crashing into Springtime Square, they overturned tables and upset sacks and ruined all of the springtime supplies that the nature talents had been preparing for weeks!

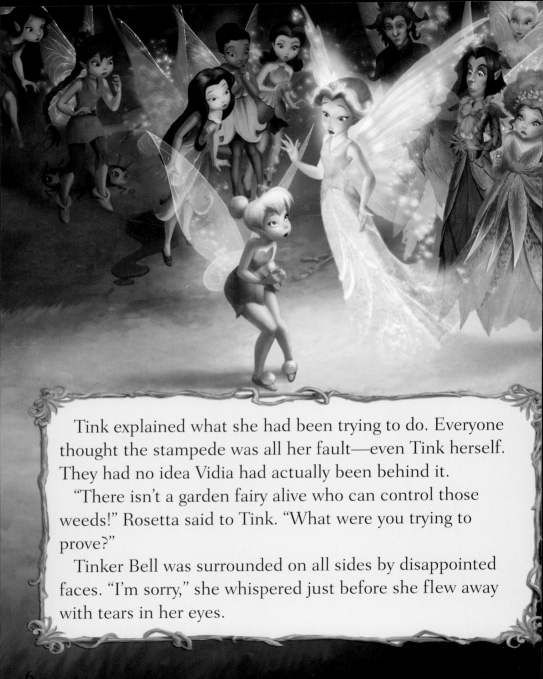

Tink explained what she had been trying to do. Everyone thought the stampede was all her fault—even Tink herself. They had no idea Vidia had actually been behind it.

"There isn't a garden fairy alive who can control those weeds!" Rosetta said to Tink. "What were you trying to prove?"

Tinker Bell was surrounded on all sides by disappointed faces. "I'm sorry," she whispered just before she flew away with tears in her eyes.

Now Queen Clarion wasn't sure what to do about spring. With all the supplies destroyed, the fairies weren't ready to bring it to the mainland.

"We're going to have to cancel the season this year," said the Minister of Spring, "or postpone it at the very least."

Meanwhile, Tinker Bell was getting ready to leave Pixie Hollow. After the mess she'd just caused, wouldn't that be the best thing—for her and for everyone else?

Tink visited the workshop in Tinkers Nook one last time. She had had fun here, even if the contraptions she'd tried to make for the nature talents had not worked. As she looked around, she saw light reflecting off something in the corner of the room. She went to get a closer look.

"Lost Things!" she said, picking up a spring, a gear, and then a screw. She had found them on the beach her first day in Never Land. Clank and Bobble had said they weren't useful for much.

But Tinker Bell had an idea. She thought this "junk" might just save spring.

That night, Queen Clarion gathered all the fairies to tell them spring would not be coming that year. But Tinker Bell stopped her. "Wait!" she cried. "I know how we can fix everything!" Tink demonstrated how she had improved her paint sprayer using Lost Things. As the fairies watched, Tink used it to paint a ladybug in seconds—a job that usually took a painting fairy fifteen minutes! And Tink had plans to make more time-saving inventions. "Making paint, gathering seeds—we can do it all in a snap!" exclaimed Tink.

Vidia urged the other fairies not to listen to Tink. But then Queen Clarion discovered Vidia's involvement in the thistle stampede. She sent Vidia off to recapture all the runaway weeds.

The fairies agreed that Tinker Bell's plan was worth a try.
Tink asked them to gather twigs, tree sap, and all the Lost
Things they could find. Then she showed them how to put
all the pieces together. She made a berry squasher that could
squeeze bucketloads of berry paint out of several berries
in an instant! She made a seed vacuum that could gather
dozens of seeds, then shoot them back out into the fairies'
buckets and sacks.

Then the fairies got to work using Tink's inventions. With their new tools, the fairies' work went faster than they ever thought possible! Long lines of ladybugs got their red base coats and black spots in the blink of an eye. Seeds were vacuumed up from all corners of Pixie Hollow. Bucket after bucket was filled to the brim with berry paint.

But the minutes were ticking by. Would they have everything ready in time for the blooming of the Everblossom—the signal that it was time to go to the mainland?

The next morning, Queen Clarion flew down into Springtime Square—and could not believe what she saw. Not only were the supplies plentiful for the fairies' trip, there were more than she had ever seen for any previous spring!

The Everblossom had bloomed, and all was ready. It was time to bring springtime to the world!

"You did it, Tinker Bell," said the queen.

"We all did it," Tink replied.

Tinker Bell was so happy. And her day was about to get even better! Clank and Bobble brought out a lovely music box Tink had repaired a few days before, and Fairy Mary praised Tink's tinkering abilities. "I imagine there's someone out there who's missing this," Fairy Mary said. "Perhaps a certain tinker fairy has a job to do after all…on the mainland."

Tink was overjoyed. She—a tinker fairy—was going to the mainland for spring!

The fairies left right away. With the help of their bird friends, they carried all the springtime supplies with them. And when they got to the mainland, they discovered they would need everything they had brought. Snow, ice, and frost covered the ground and trees, and the sky was cloudy and gray.

They fanned out in all directions and got to work. Light
fairies melted the snow and frost and created a rainbow that
arched across the bright blue sky. The animal fairies woke
the hibernating animals. Flower fairies and painting fairies
added color everywhere.

Tinker Bell watched in amazement as the world was
completely transformed.

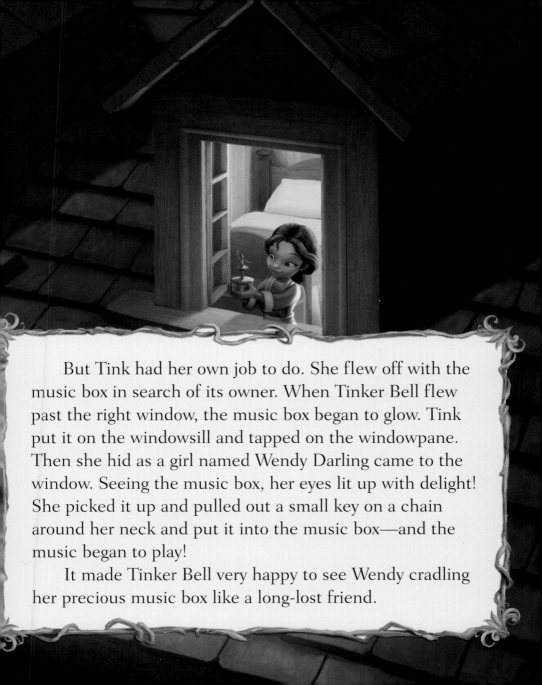

But Tink had her own job to do. She flew off with the music box in search of its owner. When Tinker Bell flew past the right window, the music box began to glow. Tink put it on the windowsill and tapped on the windowpane. Then she hid as a girl named Wendy Darling came to the window. Seeing the music box, her eyes lit up with delight! She picked it up and pulled out a small key on a chain around her neck and put it into the music box—and the music began to play!

It made Tinker Bell very happy to see Wendy cradling her precious music box like a long-lost friend.

Before Tink knew it, it was time for the fairies to head home to Never Land and end their magical journey.

From that night on, Tinker Bell never doubted that tinkering was her true talent. And she wouldn't have wanted it any other way!